Nat the Crab

by Alice Cary
illustrated by Doug Cushman

Open Court Publishing Company
Chicago and Peru, Illinois

Printed in the United States of America

ISBN 0-8126-1273-6

10 9 8 7 6 5 4 3

Nat's Nap

A crab can't nap!

A crab can't nap.

A crab can tap!
A crab can snap!

A crab can spin
and spin!

A crab can sit a bit.

Nat naps!
NAT

Nat's Trip

A trip, Nat?
A trip! A trip!

A trip in a cab, Nat?
I have the map!
TAXI

Here it is, Nat!

Here is a cap.

And here is a bat.

NAT
Nat is at bat!